W9-CBR-392

For all the sons and daughters of my Cool Dude and Sweet Princess friends
—K. O.

For my niece, Skylar Rae Atkinson, and my nephew, Chase Phillip Atkinson;
as always, for my parents, William J. and Merlyn Heyer
—C. H.

For the Royal Superkids in my life, Aleix, Michael, and Joshua;
I love you guys with and without superpowers!
—S. G.

First published in the United States of America in September 2010
by Walker Publishing Company, Inc., a division of Bloomsbury Publishing, Inc.
www.bloomsburykids.com

For information about permission to reproduce selections from this book, write to
Permissions, Walker BFYR, 175 Fifth Avenue, New York, New York 10010

The Library of Congress Cataloging-in-Publication Data
O'Malley, Kevin.
Once upon a royal superbaby / written and illustrated by Kevin O'Malley ;
illustrated by Carol Heyer ; illustrated by Scott Goto.
p.   cm.
Summary: Cooperatively writing a story for school, a girl imagines a king and queen who have a baby named Sweet
Piper who can talk to birds, while a boy names the baby Strong Viper and gives him superstrength, cool wrestling
moves, and a motorcycle and sunglasses.
ISBN 978-0-8027-2164-8 (hardcover) · ISBN 978-0-8027-2165-5 (reinforced)
[1. Creative writing—Fiction. 2. Kings, queens, and rulers—Fiction. 3. Babies—Fiction.
4. Humorous stories.] I. Heyer, Carol, ill. II. Goto, Scott, ill. III. Title.
PZ7.O526On 2010   [E]—dc22   2009054216

Kevin O'Malley's illustrations created using a yellow Number 2 pencil, a good pencil sharpener,
and quality layout paper; the line art was scanned and colored using the almighty Photoshop
Carol Heyer's illustrations created using acrylic paint on canvas
Scott Goto's illustrations created using a combination of oil paints and Photoshop

Typeset in Comic Sans MS, Galahad Oldstyle Figures, Dom Casual Medium, and Frutiger 76 Black Italic
Book design by Danielle Delaney

Printed in China by Hung Hing Printing (China) Co., Ltd., Shenzhen, Guangdong
1 3 5 7 9 10 8 6 4 2 (hardcover)
1 3 5 7 9 10 8 6 4 2 (reinforced)

All papers used by Bloomsbury Publishing, Inc., are natural, recyclable products
made from wood grown in well-managed forests. The manufacturing processes
conform to the environmental regulations of the country of origin.

Once Upon A ROYAL SUPERBABY

Written and Illustrated by Kevin O'Malley

Illustrated by Carol Heyer

Illustrated by Scott Goto

WALKER & COMPANY
NEW YORK

Once again our teacher has asked us to work on a story together. This time it has to be about a king and a queen. I wrote this. . . .
Sigh. Here he goes.

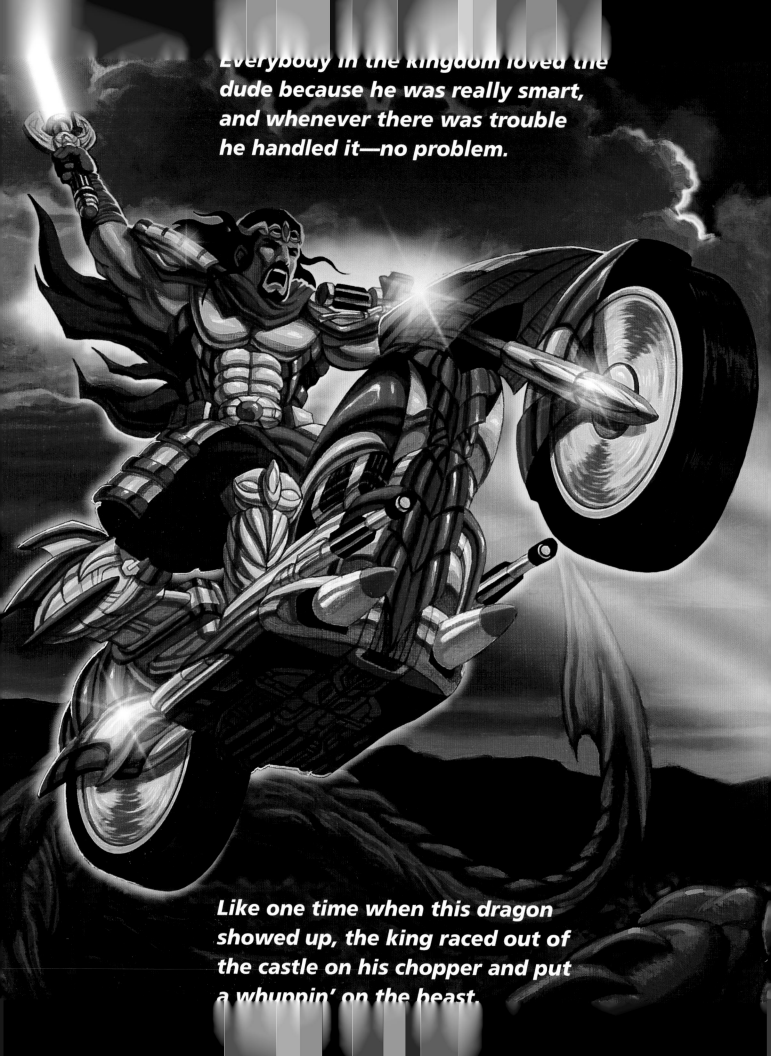

Everybody in the kingdom loved the dude because he was really smart, and whenever there was trouble he handled it—no problem.

Like one time when this dragon showed up, the king raced out of the castle on his chopper and put a whuppin' on the beast.

Queen Tenderheart decided to have a baby. The king agreed to change all the diapers.

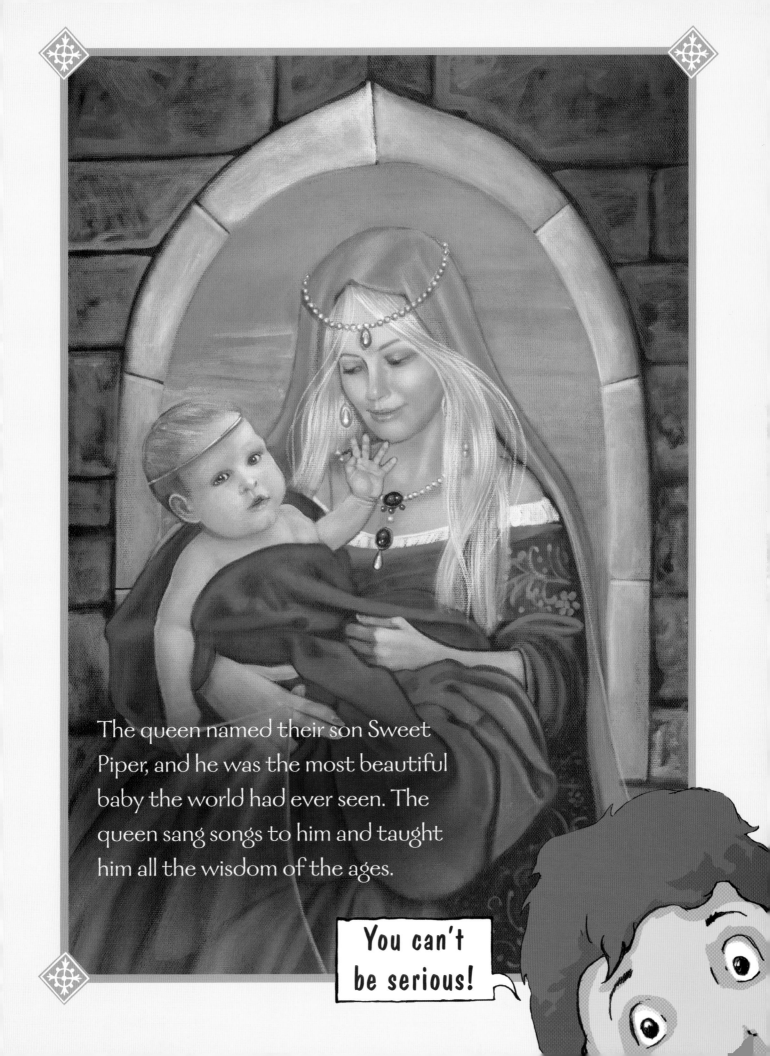

The queen named their son Sweet Piper, and he was the most beautiful baby the world had ever seen. The queen sang songs to him and taught him all the wisdom of the ages.

You can't be serious!

Sweet Piper also had a great and wonderful gift—he could speak to birds. Many times the queen would go to the nursery and find her dear baby singing songs with the little birds that flew in the window.

Talking to birds? That's not a superpower!

The king named the baby Strong Viper. He taught the baby cool wrestling moves, and all the babies at the day-care center thought he was awesome. The king even bought the baby a chopper and sunglasses.

Oh yeah, baby!

But when he needed extra power, he'd drink some juice—so he would get seriously huge muscles

One day a terrible thing happened.
An evil wizard kidnapped the king
and queen and brought them far,
far away to a dark tower that was
guarded by a gigantic cyclops.

Sweet Piper raced to the stables and jumped on the back of his mother's beautiful unicorn, Harmony. They raced through the starry night to rescue the king and queen.

The unicorn told all the animals in the forest
to help them, and together they beat the
cyclops and freed the king and queen.

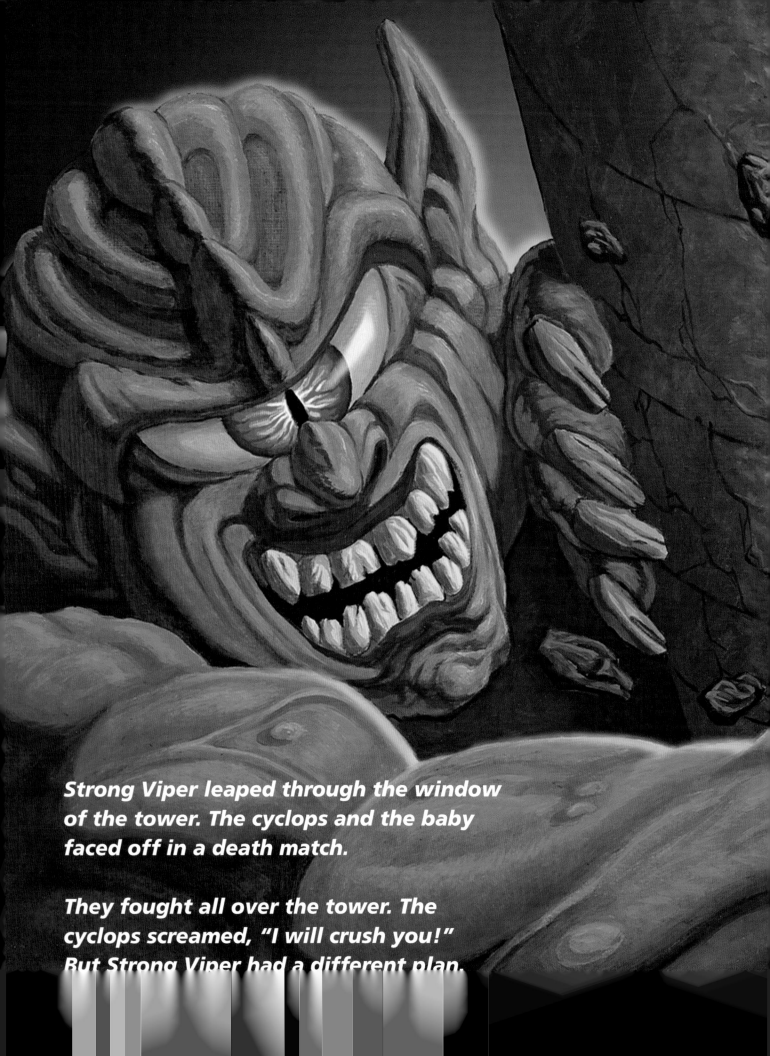

Strong Viper leaped through the window of the tower. The cyclops and the baby faced off in a death match.

They fought all over the tower. The cyclops screamed, "I will crush you!" But Strong Viper had a different plan.

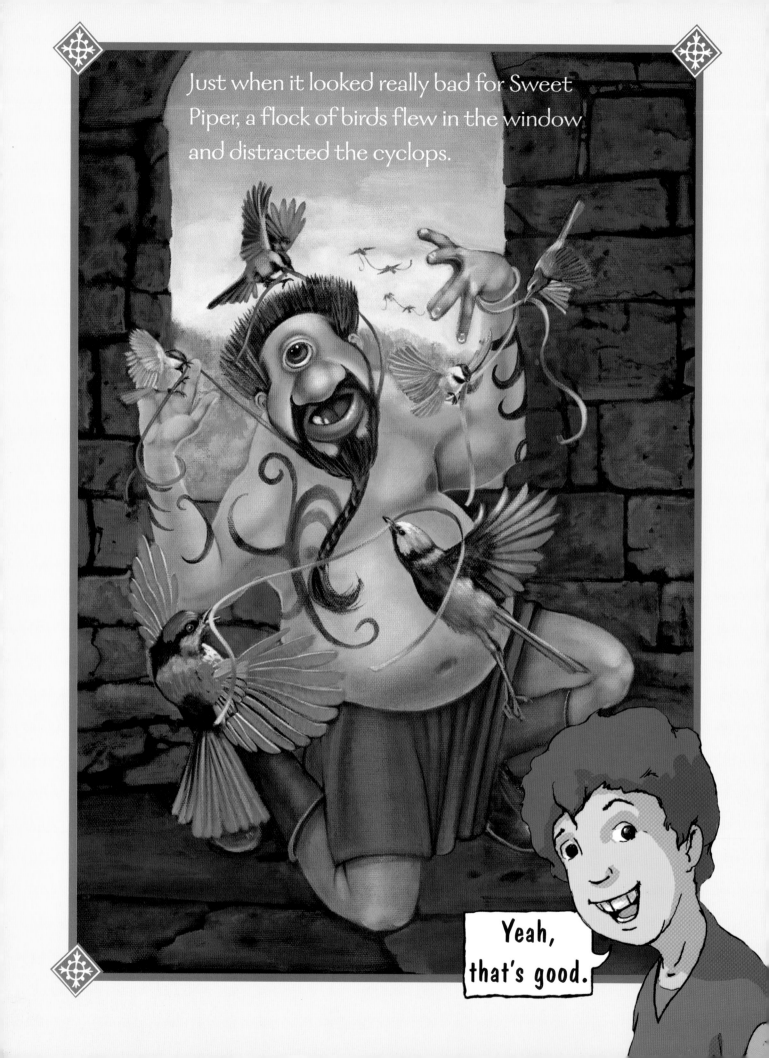

He grew very big and squirted the cyclops in the eye. And the blinded monster fell into a huge lava pit.

Excellent!

Strong Viper and his parents leaped
from the tower onto the robot
unicorn's back.

The End.